The Stray & the New Girl

Donna Soules
Illustrated by Sally Mann

THE STRAY AND THE NEW GIRL
© 2024, Donna Soules

All illustrations © 2024 by Sally Mann, except "Heart with paw prints" © 2024 by @juicy_fish on www.freepik.com.

No part of this book may be reproduced or transmitted in any form or by any means, electronic or mechanical, including photocopying, recording, or by any information storage and retrieval system, without permission in writing from the publisher, except by a reviewer, who may quote brief passages in a review.

Inquiries: Soules Consulting Ltd. (soules.ca)

Book design by Brad Grigor.

ISBN (Amazon soft cover): 978-1-9992076-1-8

PRINTED IN USA OR CANADA

*To my daughter Tonya Soules and
granddaughter Sadie Craine*

*Dedicated to all young people
and the animals they love.*

ACKNOWLEDGEMENTS

There are so many people to thank for their willingness to read, edit and encourage me to keep going with my Ralph stories.

Jennifer Franklin has spent years listening and collaborating on ideas and styles. Thanks to Sharon Styve and Cheryl Bancroft for their excellent editing, along with helpful guidance and advice from Carol Matthews and Robin McQueen. My daughter, Tonya Soules and granddaughter, Sadie Craine have given valuable time to read over this story many times — a heart-felt thank you.

My appreciation to Sally Mann who created such amazing illustrations and patiently brought to life the characters and pulled up emotions for the drawings. She somehow captured the flavour and mood I hoped for.

I want to commend Brad Grigor, the designer, for his unwavering support and steady supply of fresh ideas and wise guidance to pull this whole delightful project together.

I am grateful beyond words for the continued support of my wonderful husband who never failed me after many readings and editing suggestions.

Thank you all for your extraordinary support along this journey.

< 1 >

School: You're In or You're Out

School really sucks when I had to move from my hometown of Parksville in the spring, when all the beautiful flowers in our gardens are stunningly full of rainbow colours. And then I had to leave all my super friends behind. You move to a great new place only to find out that making new friends isn't easy. That's a problem. So, it's not really about school – it's painful going because my so-called new "friends" are hard to figure out. I get a lump in my stomach, like a moldy tomato, when I get there in the morning and I have no idea what's going on. Sometimes, they think I'm cool and I'm in, or sometimes they treat me like dog barf and I'm out. Right now, I'm barf. So mad, sad, and lonely.

I'm in a grade 5/6 split classroom. That means there are kids of different ages. Some are immature and some are more mature. This can cause competition—like who's smarter, or better liked, or older. Then you throw in the boys. They are a whole other creature. There are 26 of us in our class. Our teacher is so cool. Her name is Ms. Cook. She's a patient teacher who likes kids and her job. You can tell by the way she treats us. She travels a lot and brings some of her travel movies to class to teach us about different places. I like that. She puts time into making special events so our learning is more fun. She talks to us when she notices we're struggling with our projects. That makes me happier to learn and work harder. She dresses pretty cool too. The girls don't do anything nasty in class. Ms. Cook would have none of that smartypants stuff.

Since I now live in the country, I must take a bus to school. That's where some of my trouble started—blue lightning trouble. Before, I could walk to school from my house. When we first moved, I thought taking the bus would be fun and I'd get to know other kids faster. I sure was wrong.

< 2 >

Me and My Family

Here's a bit of news about me. Just so you know, I'm mainly a happy person. My name is Sadie, and I am 10 and the only kid in my family. I'm tall and skinny for my age, with long, light brown hair. Soccer is my game. I love it. I've played soccer since I was 5 and my parents helped me get to practice and games. I haven't found a new team yet, but Mom is working on it. Since we moved, my Dad works at the local mill. My Mom works at home doing bookkeeping. More on them later.

Another thing—I love telling stories so that's why I'm telling this one. Believe it or not, I like to listen too. To be honest, I tell stories when I'm sad and I'm sad now. As I said, going to my new school is my problem. Sometimes I tell stories when I don't want to feel lonely. When telling stories, I can go on tooooo long OR I can cut corners and leave you in the dark. I'm not going to do that. It's a deal between us, okay?

< 3 >

The New Visitor

My story tells how I made changes moving to a new school at the same time a mysterious cat also needed to make changes. It's amazing how we fixed our problems and learned together. He taught me things I needed to know, and I helped him find a new home. We listened to one another. You might wonder how I knew he was *he*. My Dad helped me with that.

The story starts at my old house in town. A street cat picked our family to live with and who knows why. I sure don't. Who can guess what a cat's thinking, right? Especially a wild cat.

On a cold spring day, this small scruffy cat, all wet from the rain, was huddled up on our back porch. He was a skittery critter. I couldn't get near him, but he sure looked sad and lonely. His fur was grey with black stripes like a tiger and his yellow eyes were fierce, like he knew trouble. When he saw me looking at him through the window, he skedaddled off the porch.

Another morning, big surprise! I went to the kitchen to get some apple juice. (Personally, I prefer apples to oranges because we have three big apple trees at our new place.) That skinny runt was inside our kitchen with both our well-fed house cats—Sid and Mukti—watching him eat their food. When he saw me, he bolted through the cat door like a super-sonic fur ball. You get the picture—animal chaos first thing in the morning, and before breakfast!

< 4 >

House Cats

Before I get ahead of myself, you might want to know about our other two cats, Sid and Mukti. They used a cat door to come and go as they pleased. They were serious guardians of that cat door and defended their kibbles jealously. Particularly from the neighbouring raccoons. Mukti, a silver-grey cat, joined our family as a kitten and she was a mittful of fun and trouble—clawing furniture, crawling up our shower curtain in the bathroom, and freaking Mom out. Mukti cracked me up. She was a loner and so curious about her own adventures. One of her tricks was to bring in snakes from the garden. One snake was soooo long she was tripping on it. When she let it go in the house, the snake crawled down into the heat duct. What a big deal to get that snake out! Mom was having guests for dinner that night in the same room. She sure didn't want a snake slithering out during the meal. With Mukti's help, we got it out—alive. I thought this was hilarious. Mom was fuming and all steamed up.

Our other cat, Sid, was a rescue cat who lived under my Auntie Olive's front porch. It wasn't her cat. He just lived there, and she fed him. At the house next door, there was a brown and black dog named Toby that terrorized Sid whenever he got the chance. The neighbours let Toby run free. I liked Toby and he scampered up to me whenever I went to my Auntie's house. Toby loved chasing cats. I never saw him catch a cat, but he sure tried hard.

Our family decided to help Sid out and brought him home to keep Mukti company. Auntie Olive was pleased about this because she felt sorry for homeless Sid. He had long black fur and a white patch under his chin. Before he came to us, my Auntie wanted to clean him up. She took him to a pet groomer who washed and combed him since his fur was all matted and dirty. When he came to our house, he looked completely different—beautiful, like a show cat. Still, he seemed freaked out by the move, his new home, and his pet salon trauma. He hid under my parents' bed for the first couple of weeks. But with time, he seemed grateful to live inside, safe from pesky old Toby the dog.

Sid was the gentlest cat ever and totally shy. As he started to relax, he would sneak into my bedroom to wake me up in the morning and gently kiss me on the cheek, or at least that's how it felt. How special was that? Sid and Mukti became best friends for me and one another.

< 5 >

The New Guy

Now, back to the new cat. I'll tell you how he got his name later. After the big surprise in the kitchen, Mukti and Sid seemed to be okay with the new cat joining the family though they kept their distance. This was unusual because you'd think they'd reject him, but they didn't. They must have felt sorry for him or something. I have to ask—do cats feel sorry about anything? What do you think?

Over the next few weeks our critters let this scrawny scaredy cat come in and chow down. They became buddies and now we have three cats. The new guy didn't like us—just the food—and we couldn't get near him yet.

< 6 >

Moving to the Country

Around this time, we had a problem—moving. We sold our house in Parksville to move 50 kilometers away to just outside Colville, in the country. That part was awesome. We were building our house on one acre of land with a forest beside the ocean with a warm water beach. I was told as fact that this harbour was the warmest body of water north of San Francisco. It sure felt like that—bathtub temperature. We also bought a second-hand inflatable boat with a motor, and a kayak. Swimming and playing in the boats were awesome. I was so excited about living there. We could also make fires on the beach and roast hot dogs and marshmallows. There were lots of big trees and two of the trees were 400 hundred years old. They are called "old growth" trees. I can't even imagine that many years.

The problem—we sold our house in town to someone with a big mean thug of a dog. Sorry for another dog story. I like dogs but I like cats even more. Dogs and cats just don't seem to get along unless they're raised together. Anyway, I think he was a Saint Bernard. He was big, with sloppy lips and drool running down his cheek. Yuck! Not my idea of cuddly. And he was smelly. Have you noticed cats smell great because they lick themselves all the time. They're clean. But then there are hair balls. Messy. What was going to happen to this poor bedraggled cat when he came in the cat door? Surprise! There would be a new family in the house with the drooling dog. What then? Chewed? Eaten? Yikes! Drastic measures needed.

So, I went to Dad with the puzzle. "Can we take the new cat with us?" What a treat when he said, "Sure, let's take the little guy with us. We have lots of room with all the land."

< 7 >

Cats That Talk

For the next few weeks, getting to know the "Little Guy," as we now called him, was an adventure. We never discovered where he was from or if he had a family. He seemed abandoned like an orphan. We could tell he was hungry, frightened, and lonely. He must have been good at dumpster diving to find food, but still he was so darn skinny. He was a real character and a survivor who needed to be rescued. This was my opinion.

Here's where it gets interesting. Are you ready?

A few days before we moved, I checked the back porch. The Little Guy heard me and came running up the stairs to meow hello. I bent down but couldn't touch him yet because he was still afraid of people. You can't blame him.

Now this part is weird. I have never had a cat talk to me, besides "Meow, meow, I'm hungry." "So, what's your name?" I asked. Get this, out of the blue the name "Ralph" flashed into my head. Ralph it was. I asked Ralph if he wanted to come and live with us at our new place near Colville and he looked up at me with eyes that said, "You bet!" Who says cats can't talk?

< 8 >

Moving Day

We made plans to take Ralph with us after we cleaned up at the house. Mom bought an extra-large cat cage to give Ralph a safe place for the trip in the van. No way would we risk him travelling with one of the other two cats in their cages. Too many bad possibilities.

When I went outside the next day and called him, Ralph came running down the lane and dashed through the open door to the living room. It was empty except for me and Dad. I had never touched Ralph, so I asked for Dad's help to put him in the cage. I was sure Ralph would freak out.

Dad was stressed from moving and had forgotten his promise to take the strange cat with us. He snapped at me! "No way can I deal with that now. We don't need another pet anyways. Just forget it. We have way too much to handle now." Bummer, Dad. I was more than disappointed because Dad didn't usually go back on his word. I couldn't handle the thought of leaving Ralph behind. I was sure he'd be so happy at Colville with all the freedom and no other dogs or fighting cats.

This was serious! Ralph was hunched on the floor looking up at us while we talked about his future. I yelled at Dad, "Then you tell him he can't come!" I was choked.

Then, an amazing thing happened. Ralph stood up and slowly walked over to Dad. He looked up as if he were begging for a home. Then he rubbed himself on Dad's leg! Can you believe it? A first! I repeated, not so upset this time, "Go ahead, you tell him he can't come."

My Dad started to melt, looked up at the ceiling, and said, "Ok, he can come." Yippee! I love you, Dad.

Let me tell you, moving Ralph wasn't easy! After much clawing and scratching, Ralph was stuffed into the cage. My brave Dad got a few scratches from that. During the trip, I kept telling Ralph he was going to be just fine; he was going to his new home. He yowled, hollered, and banged his head against the bars of the cage like a furious tiger. He frightened us and we wondered if we'd done the right thing to take him away from the neighbourhood he knew, even though it wasn't a great place for him.

< 9 >

Cabin Living

Our new home wasn't ready for us to move into yet, so we lived in our funky cabin overlooking the ocean. Through all these changes, Ralph seemed to be getting used to us. I was patient and moved very slowly around him. He still didn't trust people. I guess it takes time to fit into a new situation. He had been homeless, kicked around, chased, and attacked so he was scared and jumpy. He survived by being a fighter. Trust had to be on his terms, and he clawed Dad's arm when he tried to pick him up too soon. Dad thought that maybe he didn't like men because they had been mean to him. Kind of a warning for all of us, I guess. Take your time. Be patient and kind.

Slowly, Ralph began to relax. He finally let me hold him and he seemed at ease in his new home, the cabin. Best thing for him—he was fed every day.

< 10 >

Burnt Toast: Back to School

Even though I loved discovering spring at our new place, and staying in the tiny cabin, I had to go to a new school. It was hard to leave my special friends back in town. Fitting into a new school halfway through the school year, where I didn't know anyone was scary. I wondered how it felt for Ralph to move to a new place that he didn't know.

You get the picture? Here's Ralph adapting to his changes and here I am trying desperately to survive the changes at my new school and with new kids. We were in this together. Ralph was fitting in better than me. He had a family who accepted and wanted him. Sometimes my family just wanted me to get over my school problem.

Good thing Mom was so special. She helped me fit in...by taking me shopping for new clothes. Since it was still early spring and it was chilly in the mornings, I picked out a beautiful blue jacket with a fake fur collar. Talk about a creative design. The collar could come off as it got warmer. Mom was impressed. I was so grateful to Mom for buying it.

The next day I discovered how the girls treated new kids. I showed up with my new jacket that I just loved. It was so cool. At recess, one girl said to the others right in front me, "I bet she thinks she's pretty chill and look at the fake fur! It looks like she's wearing a dead animal. She probably bought it at the thrift store." They all snickered. This really stabbed my heart because Mom wanted to cheer me up and she spent a lot of money on the jacket I was so gone on. I felt like crying and wanted to just go home but decided I would never let them know how badly I felt. The rest of the day was toast—burnt toast. That night the tears came. I swaddled myself up in my soft cozy comforter and cried myself to sleep.

I soon discovered that this gang treated other girls the same way as me. It wasn't much comfort to learn it wasn't just me. Sometimes I wondered what was I doing to make this happen? It's hard not to take it personally. I sure couldn't figure it out and I wanted someone to talk to. It was lonely being in a new school with no one to hang out with.

The in-girls looked at me like I was a target. I had to fix this.

Mom never understood why I wasn't wearing my new jacket, and it was embarrassing to tell her the story about the mean girls at school. She was mad at me for choosing the jacket she spent so much money on. She told me I was a poor shopper. Hearing Mom say this made me feel worse than ever. The hurt just went deeper.

You might ask why I didn't tell Mom more about the snooty-faced girls. Since we moved, I noticed that when I talked to Mom about a problem, her way of helping was to tell me what to do. She wanted to solve the problem for me, and she seemed to think I should just get over it or it wasn't as bad as I thought. That sure didn't help, and she didn't have to live with the way they treated me. When she wanted to solve my problems, it felt like she thought I was broken, and I was just being a kid! I ended up feeling judged and sulked in my little cubby-hole in the cabin. Mom didn't get that I wanted to fix this myself.

< 11 >

Visit to an Old Friend

One night, I texted my close friend Amanda from Parksville, the town we moved from. I missed her so much. She is caring. I could tell her anything. She didn't blab. She made me feel like I was snuggling in a warm furry blanket. She made me smile. As you can imagine, I wasn't smiling lately. Amanda asked her mom if I could go to her house for a weekend sleepover. The moms were all for it and our plan gave me something to look forward to. I counted the days off on my bedside calendar and added a big red heart on the Friday we would get together.

We had a great time staying up late and eating popcorn. I told Amanda how upset I was and gave her the scoop on the mean kids I called "meaniors." Amanda didn't tell me what to do; she just listened and said that the situation sucked. I felt better, or at least understood. After that, we texted each other often and that helped a lot.

< 12 >

Vacation Adventure

While the new house was still not finished, our family went on a summer vacation for two weeks. Our new neighbour David fed all three cats while we were away. He was a good guy and gave them piles of kibbles.

It was good to take a break from school and squeeze the bad parts out of my head like toothpaste! We decided to go camping at Cougar Creek.

We started out thinking camping would be a treat. We were tired from packing, moving, and finishing the house. It was hard to live in the cramped space of the cabin. We were all happy to feel the warmer weather coming and see the sunshine through the trees and reflect off the sparkling water.

In July the weather is usually pretty good. But not this year. It rained for most of the time. The tent was old, and it leaked. Mom and Dad had a fight because the sleeping bags were all wet. The campsite was swarming with mosquitoes. I had big red polka dot bites all over. Mom wanted to go back to the cabin. She thought the cabin was already enough like camping. Dad wanted to stay and tough it out. Dad was having a hard time at work and building a house at the same time put things way over the top. We decided—no, Dad decided—to stay for the whole two weeks, and we did get a few nice days in the end. Sad to say, the camping trip was a bust. Not what we needed.

When we came back to our cabin, we did get a nice surprise. Ralph was no longer a scrawny little runt. He looked more like a furry watermelon with feet. Ralph lived outside while we were away, and David left him full bowls of cat food every day. Sid and Mukti stayed inside because we were afraid they would run away. We hoped Ralph wouldn't disappear but had to take that chance.

After we came home, we took Ralph to the vet to get him checked out and learned he was 2 ½ years old! The vet said he was healthy even though he had been abandoned for so long. We felt sad that Ralph must have been super hungry when he first found us.

< 13 >

Our New House

After the camping disaster, the house was ready to move into. We were all delighted. I was excited to have a beautiful new room. Everyone was happy with how the house turned out. Just the right size and we were relieved the whole project of building a house was over. We soon settled in, and slowly relaxed.

The house had a wonderful window seat facing the ocean. While I was sitting in the window seat,

Ralph jumped up on my lap. He seemed okay in the new house after a few months passed. I was reading a book for school and petting him at the same time. Whenever I gave him my full attention and stroked Ralph gently, he would purr. But if I didn't

give him 100% attention, he bit me. Ouch! It hurt! This was not the first time he did it. Pretty nasty stuff and I didn't like it. He was getting bigger and stronger, and his more aggressive wild side was coming out.

This time, I jumped up and in a loud voice, I yelled at him. "Ralph, if you EVER bite me like that again, I will put you in a box and take you back to your dumpster in Parksville. You'll have no food, no love, and no home. Now get outside and think about it." He never bit me again.

When I told her what I had done, Mom said it was good to put my boundaries in place. That was a new idea. I said, "What do you mean—boundaries?" "Well," she said, "you know how your room is a special place for you to go and you don't like people barging in? So, when people or animals do things you don't like, they're crossing your boundary. It's like drawing a line in the sand. You let them know you are not okay if they cross it." Humm…that sure gave me something to think about.

< 14 >

Sleep-over Gone Bad

After we were all moved into the house and school had started again in September, Mom said I could invite four girls from my new school for a sleep-over. She thought this might help us get to know each other. Mom made pizzas with lots of cheese and sauce, a big jug of juice and a huge bowl of popcorn. She rented a movie online called *The Magician's Cat*. I thought the girls would like it.

The party was going well, then Ralph padded into the TV room and jumped into my lap to check things out. We hadn't finished the movie when they started to make fun of Ralph for being so fat. They called him "Meatball" and "Lardo." They joked and said that when he ran, his stomach swung like a hammock. I guess that was true. They laughed because we had to change the cat door to a dog door because Ralph couldn't fit through the cat door. I yelled at them, "What!!! You're hurting his feelings and mine too." I was mad and wanted their nastiness to stop. I wanted to swear a red streak at them but thanks to Mom's lessons of good manners, I reined myself in. The girls wanted to leave, and we didn't finish the movie. One of the girls named Emma said she was sorry when she left. The sleep-over idea was a bust. What a drag. To make matters worse, someone made a post on social media about my stupid sleep-over.

< 15 >

More School Nightmares

After that, I wanted to stop going to school. Over the weekend, I was hurt and sad and ready to give up. First, they're mean to me and now they're mean to my cat. My heart just couldn't take it. I didn't understand why they would treat me so badly. What did they get out of all the put-downs? And my cat, too, if you can believe it.

This was the first time Mom saw how these so-called friends were acting. We talked about it at bedtime, and she offered to help, but I told her I wanted to fix the problem myself. She wanted to go to the school and tell the principal about what was happening with these girls, but I said, "No way!" That would only make it worse. You can imagine them joking that I needed my mommy to rescue me. Maybe they wouldn't be mean to me anymore—they'd just hate me, and I'd never be able to work it out.

There was a counsellor at the school named Ms. Nelson who taught a class in life skills, and she seemed nice. I thought I might check her out one day, but right then, I couldn't face that stuff until I felt better. It all seemed so hopeless.

< 16 >

Ralph Mischief

Because of the troubles at school, Ralph became my new focus, to try and help him when I was making such a muck of things at school. I was embarrassed. People could see I was having a hard time and feeling miserable. I often walked around wearing a "stunned raccoon face." That was Dad's comment. I didn't like it.

Mom worked from home, so she was around a lot. She was able to keep her bookkeeping job, but she missed her friends at work. Mom and Dad thought it best for her to keep working and help with the bills. Dad had started this new job at the mill when we moved, and at suppertime he was always complaining about how much he hated it. Now he was the new kid on the block. He was working all the time and Mom was mad about this. We hardly saw him.

One night at supper, Mom came up with the idea of having Dad's boss and wife for dinner. Dad just went along with it and invited his new boss and his wife, Mr. and Mrs. Jolly, for dinner. Mom and I hoped this would help Dad with how he felt about work.

The night was going pretty well, and Dad seemed to relax a bit. We were glad about this. Then Ralph came to the party. Ralph seemed to like Mrs. Jolly, jumped up on the couch and sat next to her. She was petting him while she talked to Mom. I worried he might bite her, but he didn't. He looked pretty content. When we all moved to the table for supper, Ralph went outside. He had learned some manners by now! After dinner, we all went back to the couches for coffee and tea. Then I noticed Ralph was sitting patiently, staring at the bookcase. Curious what Ralph was doing, I went over and looked at the bookcase too. When I looked behind the bookcase, two beady red eyes stared back at me. I yelled, and a large rat dashed beside the couch where Mrs. Jolly was sitting. She shrieked and leaped up on the couch. What a sight! Dad laughed at first. Mrs. Jolly was flapping her arms in a panic. The rat bolted down the hall. I didn't know rats could run that fast. Dad and I chased the rat with our fish net, and Ralph scrambled to keep up with his tummy flapping. He wasn't going to miss this meal. Finally, after much chaos, Dad caught the rat in our fish net while I held Ralph back. Dad carried the rat outside to freedom. "Oh, my goodness," exclaimed Mrs. Jolly. "What a rescue. That was a terrible fright for me. I've never seen a rat that big. Ralph's a great hunter but you must teach him not to bring those vile creatures into the house. Well done, you two." Dad says Mrs. Jolly still talks about that rat who came to dinner, and she never came back.

Well, you can guess that food is a big deal for Ralph. It sure makes sense that if you spend your early years eating out of dumpsters, you'd never want to be hungry again. This was a big deal for

Ralph to see it didn't make people happy when he brought a gift they didn't want: a live rat for Mrs. Jolly. Maybe he wanted to treat Mrs. Jolly to a gift she didn't like. Why would Ralph do this? "Those cats like to stir up trouble to keep things lively." Maybe Ralph learned a few tricks from Mukti, who brought snakes into the house.

< 17 >

Raccoon Story

There was one more thing Ralph and I still had to get straight. It was about a special new friend named Rocky. You guessed it, Rocky the raccoon. It was the first time I had spotted this little guy. He was sitting under the bird feeder hanging in the apple tree, eating the last dregs of the bird seed that had fallen on the ground. Rocky reminded me of Ralph when he first showed up at our back porch. He was obviously hungry if he was desperate enough to eat seeds. That's not a raccoon's diet. What do raccoons eat anyway? I looked it up online. They eat fruit, nuts, corn, fish, frogs, insects, bird eggs, rodents, dead animals, and garbage. Seeds, not so much.

Watching Rocky snoop around for more food, I noticed he was limping. I found a tin pie plate in the recycle bin and filled it with cat kibbles. Well, this was ringing alarm bells for Ralph, who was sitting on the back deck watching Rocky. A serious talk with Ralph was called for once again. I sat down with him and said, "Here's the drill." I was confident Ralph would listen to me. I told him Rocky was also my friend. He was injured and needed my help. I gave strict orders not to go after Rocky. He couldn't chase him or attack him. I added one exception—if Rocky came on the deck or tried to get into the house through the cat door, Ralph could chase him off the deck, but that was all. Ralph just sat there looking out at Rocky under the tree eating his dinner. I guess I just gave Ralph another boundary. I think I'm getting the hang of boundaries.

Then I got a lecture from Dad. He said, "You can't feed that raccoon. He's a wild animal and raccoons can be fierce. Feeding him will encourage him to come into the house by the cat door. Can you picture the mess in here with a wild raccoon tearing things apart. No way!"

Then a friend of my parents came to visit, and he heard the story from me. He said, "You're already feeding the raccoon with the bird seed, so what's the difference?" I told him about the rules

I gave Ralph about guarding the deck and the cat door. He laughed. So far, Ralph had been on patrol duty and making sure Rocky would stay outside. I was allowed to feed Rocky after that. Seemed to me that parents listened more to other adults than their own kids! Go figure.

Next, a huge delight. Rocky had feasted and was looking much better with no limp, but we discovered that Rocky wasn't "Rocky"—she was a female! We renamed her Rockette. We discovered she had made a nest high up in the crook of a cedar tree near the beach. After disappearing for a month, she returned to her tin plate to eat and, to our surprise, out of the bushes came 5 baby raccoons running after her. Baby raccoons are called kits. We were thrilled. This worried me as Ralph could definitely go after one of her babies. And yes,

Ralph and I needed to have another chat. To our amazement, Ralph kept this deal and he never harmed any of the raccoons that whole summer.

After the fall season, we never saw Rockette again. We did see three young raccoons come to the apple tree. They looked strong and healthy, and I didn't need to feed them.

< 18 >

A New Plan

Back at school, after the sleepover, I was still 'out' with the girls. They appeared as a herd around their leader. They were telling everyone what a stupid sleepover they had at my place, that my cat was gross and fat. They were all laughing. They hated the movie and thought it was stupid—a little kid's movie. I was embarrassed, sad and mad. I walked away so I didn't have to listen to them. I felt like crying, and I sure didn't want anyone to see that.

After falling asleep later that night, I suddenly woke up and groaned, "That's **enough**!" Their meanness was just like Ralph biting my arm. I rehearsed doing the same thing with my so-called friends that I did with Ralph. If yelling at Ralph to stop biting worked a couple of months ago, maybe it would work with these nasty catty girls. If someone bites you, you bite them back, right? Then I thought about how this would work. I realized you can't talk to people the way you talk to a cat. Yelling at these girls would not be a picnic for anyone. I wanted to be more mature and say how I honestly felt.

I went to them at recess the next day and said, "I don't like the way you're treating me. The things you say and do are hurtful. I don't like it and if you treat me like that again, I'm no longer willing to be around you." I walked away. I said my piece and I was finished. I guess I wanted to put my boundaries in place with these girls at school. Thanks Mom.

Two days later, Emma, one of the girls from the group who said she was sorry the night of the sleepover, came up to me and said it must have taken a lot of courage to say that to them. She added, "I'm not into those games either." She was so kind we decided to be friends. We made a pact that if we EVER had problems with each other we would talk about it, fix it, and not walk away. I made a real friend that day. This was the first time I felt happy at that school and had some hope for a better time. I almost cried for joy.

You might have noticed I haven't shared these other girls' names with you. I think I just didn't want to give them any of my attention.

We still had this problem, so Emma and I decided to go and see Ms. Nelson. She was very kind and let us know she understood how hard this change in schools was for me. Emma didn't say much. She let me talk and explain the problem. Ms. Nelson asked if it would help us to know a bit about these girls. She said they had sad stories too. She was careful not to mention names or to say too much about their personal problems.

What little she did tell us made me stop and think what a good home life I had. How my parents took such good care of me—loved me. Yes, my parents had problems too, and they seemed to work them out. Some girls had both parents working and didn't get much care or attention at home. There was a lot of conflict in their families. I noticed that one girl had the whole front of her hair cut off. It was a mess. She told Ms. Nelson her stupid older brother and his friend did it as a joke when she was sleeping on the couch. Another girl's mother had left the family, and her father was looking after her and two younger kids. He had a new girlfriend they didn't like. It didn't sound like a happy home. If somebody is mean, maybe there is other stuff going on for them. Underneath their meanness, they might feel hurt or angry and wanted to take the hurt out on someone else. That thought was new for me.

< 19 >

Seeking Help

This whole discussion with Ms. Nelson was a wake-up call for me. Emma already knew some of the issues with the other girls' families, but I had no idea they had any problems. I now realized they were hurting too. It sure made me think differently about them. I didn't like how they treated me, but I saw more of the whole picture. Some of their nastiness wasn't about me. It was about their own stuff.

Now, I feel sad for them. They seemed to think bad attention was better than no attention, or at least that's how I thought about it.

After a couple of months passed, Ms. Nelson called Emma and me to her office at recess. She was checking in to see how things were going. I hung my head and told her nothing had changed. She told us about a special group that met once a month—a few boys and girls get together and talk about how students treat each other. The group is called "No Blame," and the focus is on resolving conflicts.

Ms. Nelson told us a sad story about a girl named Jaz who had moved to Canada from India the year before. Ms. Nelson told us Jaz had given her permission to tell us her story. Jaz joined this group to try to work things out. With the support of the group, she became a really positive person who learned a lot about helping other students get along. Ms. Nelson said that Jaz's problems with the other girls resolved themselves in a couple of weeks.

Ms. Nelson asked if we were up for a new experience and would we like to give the meeting a try. Emma and I looked at each other and we agreed to try it out. She also told us she had invited the other girls I was having problems with, and they agreed to join too. We were surprised they wanted to join the group.

The meeting happened the following week. Jaz's grandmother made Indian food called momos for the kids to try during the meeting. Momos are pastries that look like dumplings. They are prepared with ground beef, potatoes, and onions. They were yummy. I liked them.

We all listened to Jaz tell her story about the difficult time she had adjusting to all the changes she had gone through. She said other students saw her as different and treated her badly. They made fun of the way her weird food smelled and joked about her accent. Jaz decided not to go to school and told her parents she was sick. Jaz admitted there was some truth to this, as she did feel sick about school and being teased about her clothes, accent, and her lunch.

Her teacher sent a note to Jaz's parents about homework. She had missed a week of school by now. That was when Ms. Nelson got involved and invited her to the "No Blame" group.

With Ms. Nelson's and Jaz's care and support, other kids in the group shared stories too. I was amazed to hear that some of the boys had the same problems as me. This made it easier for me to share how I felt, and no one was blamed for the problems. When other students heard about how comments can be so hurtful, I really felt that things had changed.

After the meeting, Emma and I felt better about hanging out with the other girls sometimes. The nasty comments stopped. We would talk about the weekend or play baseball at recess with them. I think they understood me a bit more too. If someone did say something that wasn't so nice, I felt comfortable asking them why they said that. I didn't get hurt or mad, I just got curious. It seemed there was more comfort among us. It was like the meeting gave me a new road map to deal with the other girls at school. I felt stronger. When I saw them, it didn't feel like I was going over a speed bump.

< 20 >

Finding Hope

It was a gift to have a friend like Emma, someone I could count on. I liked her and felt she liked me too. It was so nice to relax, feel more comfortable, and not always be on the lookout. We did fun things together and hung out at recess. After school, we walked home together and spent time at each other's houses. Our moms were happy for us and glad to see us together. The No Blame meeting really helped us.

One other thing happened—I didn't have an upset stomach or hate school anymore. I looked forward to my days there. Even my grades got better since I wasn't so worried about the other girls.

An even bigger surprise is hearing myself giving you all their names. This feels good and I think I have made a change in how I am reacting to finding my place at school. Here's what I discovered about them. Ivy is a very good baseball player. She can hit a home run by dashing like a leopard. It was cool to watch her long brown ponytail bounce when she flew around the bases. Sally loves to draw. She is a volunteer on the school newsletter, and she is the youngest on the team. I never knew that about her. Trina likes to cook since her mom left. She helps her dad out a lot with cooking. Her favourite meal is tacos. Somehow these three girls look different to me, in a good way.

I was delighted when Mom found a soccer club I could join in our new hometown of Colville, so now I have practice on Monday and Thursday and a game on Sunday. It is super fun to be playing again and getting good workouts. The team has good coaching, and we're winning games. I like my coaches and am meeting some great new friends.

I started to wear my cool jacket again in the fall. I really do love it. It reminds me of Ralph. Mom's happy too.

Ralph's doing just fine living and scouting on his new place. He has even started to play when you tease him with a toy on a string. He never knew how to play—he didn't have that chance before. He is happy to be in our family.

We learned some things together: patience, don't give up on what you want, and with time, changes are not so bad.

Love is a serious mystery.

DISCUSSION QUESTIONS FOR PARENTS OR TEACHERS TALKING WITH CHILDREN ABOUT CONFLICT

Please select questions from the list below that are appropriate for the young people you are talking with.

- What do you think Sadie's conflict was about? What caused it?
- What was Sadie feeling?
- What do you think about how Sadie managed her conflict with the other girls at school?
- What do you think the other girls thought about Sadie?
- What were the other girls feeling?
- How much was Sadie a problem for them?
- When you think about the other girls, what conflicts did they have in life?
- What did Sadie learn that helped her deal with these conflicts?
- What else could Sadie have done to solve the problem with the girls?
- What do think about Emma and the choices she made?
- What conflicts do you have that trouble you at home or school?
- What kinds of problems do you have with your friends?
- How many other students or friends that you know felt like Sadie?
- How did they solve their problems?
- If you were having difficulty with other students, what

would stop you from talking about it?
- What help would you need and whom would you turn to?
- What resources are available to you? (parents, teachers, friends)
- How do your teachers at school handle conflict?
- How are conflicts at home handled?
- How did the "No Blame" group help Sadie and the other students?
- How would this story be different if it concerned conflicts with a mix of genders?
- What are your thoughts on how Sadie managed Ralph's biting behaviour?
- What did you like about Ralph?

REFERENCES

- Article by Michaela Haas. January 8, 2024. A Surprising Way to Stop Bullying
- Google: Bettina Denervaud on "No-Blame" approach to bullying in schools.
- Understanding Conflict: Bridging Theory and Practice, Soules Consulting Ltd. Available on Amazon.

ABOUT THE AUTHOR

Donna Soules has been a counselor in an alternate high school and has worked in a forensic adolescent treatment center with youth from ages 11 to 17. She has taught conflict resolution skills to many school children of all ages. She has been working in the field since 1991 and is currently a mediator and educator. She lives with her husband in Ladysmith, BC.

ABOUT THE ILLUSTRATOR

Sally Mann was born in Liverpool, UK. She went to Cardiff Art College in the sixties and Wrexham Art College in the nineties studying ceramic design. She loves drawing, painting, and making "whimsical" sculptures from papier-mâché. She has lived on Vancouver Island for 19 years and is an active member of the Ladysmith and Chemainus art scene.

Made in the USA
Middletown, DE
09 September 2024